This book belongs to:

Shawn Sheep
The Soccer Star

Story by Erin Mirabella

Illustrations by Sarah Davis

VELO press

Boulder, Colorado

S hawn Sheep and the rest of the Barnsville Sports Squad sat in the stands watching a professional soccer match between the Lacoochee Comets and the Dundee Dinos.

"Go, Comets!" Shawn shouted.

His all-time favorite player, Paul the Peacock, played for the Comets.
Down on the field, Paul's teammate passed him the ball.
"Shoot it!" Shawn screamed from the stands as he jumped up and down.
Paul kicked the ball past the goalie.
"Yippee!" Shawn cheered. "What a shot!"

Paul strutted around, flexing his muscles.

"Who's the best?" he shouted.

"I'm the best!"

He did the peacock power dance for the crowd. Then he yelled, "You Dinos are on your way to being extinct!"

He is so cool, Shawn thought.

"He looks silly, and he's such a bigmouth," Dana Duck said.

Gracie Goat agreed. "Yeah, his teammates helped him. He didn't score that goal all by himself."

Shawn didn't hear them.

He was too busy doing flips in the walkway.

After the game, Coach took the team to the Spaghetti House for dinner. Shawn couldn't stop talking about Paul the Peacock.

While Coach talked to the team, Shawn daydreamed about scoring the winning goal, just like Paul. He practiced the foot moves for the peacock power dance under the table. He accidentally kicked Dana.

"Ouch!" she cried. She scowled and kicked him back.

"Listen up," said Coach. "Tomorrow is a big game for us. If we win, we'll be in the league finals. Let's eat a good meal and get a good night's sleep so we'll be ready.

"And remember, *how* we win is just as important as winning. Let's have fun tomorrow and play a game we can be proud of."

A big crowd came the next morning to watch the game between the Barnsville Sports Squad and the Sand City Suns.

Before the game, Coach called the team together for their cheer.

"RUN, DRIBBLE, SHOOT, SCORE. We like to win and we're back for more!

"Gooooo Barnsville."

"Go get 'em!" said Coach.

"The sun's about to set, Sand City. You are going down!" Shawn shouted across the field. He thought he was almost as clever as Paul the Peacock. He smacked his gum loudly and blew a big bubble.

Dana popped it. "Why don't you worry about playing?" she said. Shawn ignored her and blew another bubble.

The referee blew the whistle to start the game. Shawn spit out his gum and ran onto the field with the other players.

With less than ten minutes left, the game was tied 2 to 2.

A Suns player took a shot at Barnsville's goal. Dougie Dog dove and caught the ball in midair.

Dougie threw the ball back in to Gracie. A Suns player came after the ball, and Gracie passed it to Chelsea Chicken. Chelsea dodged another player and dribbled down the field. She passed the ball to Peter Pig.

Peter charged down the field toward the Suns' goal. He was almost there when two players blocked his path.

Peter thought quickly and kicked the ball across the field to Shawn. Shawn jumped up and headed the ball into the goal.

The referee blew the whistle. "Goal!" he yelled.
The Barnsville fans cheered.
Shawn pumped his fist.

"Who's the best?" he shouted.
"I'm the best!"

He did the peacock power
dance, just like Paul.

The rest of the team watched
Shawn take all of the credit.

Dana ruffled her feathers.
Peter shrugged. Rebecca Rabbit
gave Shawn a dirty look.

"Okay, enough of that," the
referee warned Shawn.

As the teams lined up at midfield, Shawn smiled. He knew he was the best player on the team.

"Your goalie's not so hot. I bet that burns you up," Shawn yelled to the Suns.

The referee blew the whistle, and play started.

Shawn wasn't paying attention. "I'm the one on fire here."

"Your ball, Shawn!" Peter called.

Shawn turned as the ball went flying past him.

One of the Suns got the ball and took off.

"What's wrong with you?" Peter asked him.

"Keep your head in the game, Shawn!" Coach called from the sideline.

Shawn watched as the Suns wove up the field and scored a goal. Their fans cheered.

Shawn was embarrassed. "You got lucky!" he shouted at the Suns.

The game was tied again.

A few minutes later, Howard Horse passed Shawn the ball. Shawn trapped it, but as it dropped to the ground it hit his hand.

The referee blew the whistle. "Hand ball," he said.

"What?" Shawn yelled.

"I didn't touch it!"

The referee blew his whistle again. "Yellow card," he said, holding up the card. "You need to show some respect," he told Shawn.

"Are you blind?" Shawn argued.

"That's it," said the referee. He held up a red card. "You're out of the game."

Shawn was shocked. He stomped over to the bench.

Coach looked very unhappy.

"The hand ball was an accident, Coach," Shawn explained.

"The hand ball didn't get you kicked out of the game," replied Coach. "We'll talk later."

Shawn looked over at his mom and dad in the stands. They looked disappointed.

The game was almost over.

Rebecca dribbled the ball downfield. One of the Suns tried to steal the ball, but Rebecca hopped to the left and passed it to Dana.

The clock was ticking, but Dana kept her cool. She took a shot on goal.

The Suns' goalie dove to the side and knocked the ball away.

Suddenly Peter stepped up and kicked the ball into the goal.

Time was up. The referee blew the whistle ending the game.

The Barnsville Sports Squad had won!

The Barnsville fans cheered. Coach ran out onto the field and hugged his team. Everyone celebrated.

"Great shot, Peter!" said Dana.

"Thanks." Peter beamed. "You and Rebecca were awesome!"

Shawn ran onto the field and tried to give Dana a high five.

"You have got to be kidding me. You were so rude today," she said.

Howard agreed. "She's right, Shawn. What is with your attitude?"

Shawn was surprised. "We won! Aren't you happy? We're going to the finals!" he said.

Coach stepped in. "I'm sorry, Shawn, but after the way you behaved today, you won't be playing in the finals."

Shawn couldn't believe it. "But I'm the best player on the team," he said.

"How we win is more important than winning, Shawn," said Coach. "You know my rules."

Shawn sulked off the field. The rest of his team lined up to slap hands with the Suns.

On the way home, Shawn's parents stopped at a gas station. In the parking lot there was a big van with COMETS on the side. Shawn couldn't believe it. Maybe Paul the Peacock was inside the shop.

Shawn grabbed a pen and ran inside. He gasped. There was Paul the Peacock! He was taller than he looked on TV.

Shawn ran up to him. "You're the best!" he blurted.

"Go away, kid," Paul said as he filled a cup with soda.

"Will you sign my jersey?" Shawn asked, holding out his pen.

"No, kid, I'm busy. Now get lost," Paul said.

As Paul turned to leave, his drink slipped out of his grasp. It fell to the floor and splashed all over.

Shawn was soaked with soda.

Paul said a lot of bad things, but he didn't say "Sorry," and he didn't clean up the mess. He just walked out of the shop. Shawn couldn't believe it.

Shawn walked slowly back to the car. The soda made his shorts stick to his legs.

Paul may be a good soccer player, but he sure acts like a jerk! he thought. *I don't want to be like him anymore.*

Then he remembered some of the things he had yelled during the game.

He felt awful.

The next day Shawn went to practice. He had something to tell his team. "I want to say sorry for the way I acted yesterday."

The team looked surprised.

"It's okay," Dougie said.

Dana playfully punched Shawn's shoulder. "We forgive you," she said.

Everyone agreed.

Shawn looked at Coach. "I know I can't play in the finals, but I'd like to be there to cheer on the team," Shawn said.

"That's a great idea," said Coach.

"Guess what? I saw Paul the Peacock at the gas station yesterday," Shawn told the team.

"No way!" said Dana.

"Did you get his autograph?" Gracie asked.

"No," Shawn said. "But he spilled his soda on me." He held out his soda-stained shorts for them to see.

They all huddled together to hear the rest of Shawn's story. From that day on, none of them were big fans of Paul the Peacock.

Especially not Shawn.

And he never did the peacock power dance again.

All About Soccer

Soccer is the most popular sport in the world. The Olympic Games and World Cup are the two most important soccer events. In the United States the sport is called soccer, but in most countries it is called football.

There are 11 players on a team. Each player has a different job.

Some play **offense** and try to score goals.

Others play **defense** and try to keep the other team from scoring.

The team works together to pass the ball up the field. Dribbling is when players use both feet to control and move the ball.

Sometimes players use their feet, legs, or chests to stop the ball, or trap it. Players are not allowed to touch the ball with their hands unless they are throwing it in from out of bounds.

Goalies are the only players who may use their hands all the time. When the other team takes a shot on goal, it is the goalie's job to stop the ball.

The team that scores the most goals wins.

Fitness Fact

Coach taught Shawn and his teammates that the food they eat affects how much energy they have and how healthy they are. Good foods like spaghetti and meatballs, rice and vegetables, tuna sandwiches, oatmeal and fruit, and eggs and toast give you energy that lasts a long time. Foods like chips, candy bars, and sugar cereal are "junk" foods. They give you a quick burst of energy, but it doesn't last long and can make you feel even more tired afterward. Maybe that's why Paul the Peacock was so rude!

Shawn tries to eat grains, meat or beans, dairy, vegetables, and fruits every day. Oranges are his favorite snack! He only has candy, cookies, chips, and soda every once in a while as a special treat. The Barnsville Sports Squad knows that to feel their best, they need to choose healthy foods to fuel their bodies.

For Mom, Dad, and Becca

Shawn Sheep the Soccer Star
Text copyright © 2008 by Erin Mirabella
Illustrations copyright © 2008 by Sarah Davis
All rights reserved. Printed in China.

No part of this book may be reproduced, stored in a retrieval system, or transmitted, in any form or by any means, electronic or photocopy or otherwise, without the prior written permission of the publisher except in the case of brief quotations embodied in critical articles and reviews.

For information on purchasing VeloPress books, call 800/234-8356 or visit www.velopress.com.

08 09 10 / 10 9 8 7 6 5 4 3 2 1

VELO press

1830 North 55th Street
Boulder, Colorado 80301-2700 USA
303/440-0601
Fax 303/444-6788
E-mail velopress@insideinc.com

First Edition

Design by Debbie Berne,
Herter Studio LLC, San Francisco

Distributed in the United States and Canada by Publishers Group West

Library of Congress Cataloging-in-Publication Data

Mirabella, Erin.
Shawn Sheep the soccer star / Erin Mirabella ; [illustrations by Sarah Davis].
    p. cm.
ISBN 978-1-934030-16-5 (hardcover : alk. paper)
[1. Sportsmanship—Fiction. 2. Soccer—Fiction. 3. Animals—Fiction.] I. Title.
    PZ7.M67347Shc 2008
    [E]—dc22

                                    2007050362